SEVEN
SMOOTH STONES

BILL MUIR

SEVEN
SMOOTH STONES

by Bill Muir

Seven Smooth Stones

Bill Muir

A short story for busy people & how to nurture one's Soul

Methinx Publishing
methinxentertainment.com

Printed in the United States of America
First paper edition by Methinx Publishing
ISBN: 978-1-7347696-8-5

Art & Design:
Contributing Editor: Shyann Papia
Cover Art: Digital Coast Media, LLC

The Beginning

In a bustling city, one that never seemed to slow, an exceptionally successful man had climbed the corporate ladder and made his mark on the world. He had it all—his business had never been better, his office never more significant, and his bank account never larger.

Due to his success, he was regularly invited to lunch with senators, mayors, and other elected officials. He received the best seats at every major civic and sports activities. He was in demand to speak at large national conventions.

His days were full of important meetings, one right after the other. Not a day went by that he wasn't getting things done, and that was what life was all about to him, getting things done.

After his morning workout at the private gym in his building, he put on one of his best suits and felt eyes on him as he walked to the nearest elevator. When he walked through the lobby, he looked like a man who had just finished a photo shoot for *GQ*.

When he was on the phone in his office, he would stand to remind himself how important time was and to keep conversations as short as possible. He booked his calendar two years in advance, which kept his two secretaries busy.

One fall day, he was told at the last minute that a client had to cancel a non-refundable consulting appointment with him. For an executive who charged more for one appointment than most people make in a month, he had experienced few cancellations in this season of his career.

He had the hour to himself, and for a man who was always busy, an hour alone was something special and almost foreign. He decided to sit in his office alone; it had been years since he had done anything like that.

He leaned back in his large, leather desk chair and studied the office he worked in every day. It was on the top floor of the largest building in the city. The interior was a mixture of hardwood floors, granite fireplaces, and Italian leather sofas that had won him several design awards. He had filled his office with only the most famous and expensive art one would dare keep outside a well-guarded museum. Art, he discovered that day, he never looked at.

He made sure over the years he had the best of everything, no matter what it cost: the office, desk, pictures, furniture, and sound system were both expensive and perfect in every way. That was his signature: a perfect, well-managed image.

Everything in his life was designed to reflect the man he had made himself to be, rich, powerful, and above all, successful.

So there he sat on top of the world, considered by most, as one of the most powerful individuals in the city, and surprisingly, he only thought about his rebellious sons, his bad marriage, and a house he didn't want to go home to.

"What had gone wrong?" He thought to himself.

After thinking about his family, he turned his thoughts inward and knew the problem wasn't just fractured relationships. He himself was broken. He couldn't ignore the feelings that bubbled up from this quiet moment, he was bored, stuck, and dead inside. His soul felt bankrupt, and the interior of his life was as barren as the alley behind his office.

He had decided to put all of his effort, time, and resources into material life and had nothing left for his soul. He evaluated himself that day and came up wanting something he hadn't experienced in quite some time.

At the end of that hour, he left his office and walked down the hallway to his vice president's office. He pushed the door open and, without hesitation, gave her the assignment of finding someone who could help him renovate his soul.

"Listen, I have never given you a *more* important assignment," he said, ignoring the puzzled look on her face and left her office as fast as he had come in.

The first thing the next day, the vice president handed him a piece of paper with the name of a monk who lived on the outside of the city at a small, quiet monastery.

"I hear he is really good," she said with kind assurance.

"Then cancel all my morning appointments," he said.

"What will I say to them?" Asked his assistant.

"Tell them the truth; tell them I'm refurbishing."

He immediately left his office and drove out to the monastery unannounced. Even if the monk was busy, the executive figured he could negotiate a meeting right away. He was used to getting his way.

He marched into the quiet main room of the monastery and almost knocked over a very small woman with a beautiful smile on her face and a broom in her hand.

"I'm sorry, could I see the administrative assistant for the Monk," he asked her, wiping away a few specks of dust that had gathered on his sports coat.

"I'm sorry, but you can't see her because he doesn't have an administrative assistant or a secretary for that matter. But I can take you to him right now, and you can speak to him if you want," she said, her beautiful smile remaining as she spoke.

He was caught off guard to find out that the monk was free to see him right away. *"Must not be that good if he's not busy doing it,"* thought the executive.

The lady guided him down a narrow, dimly lit hallway to an unusually small, wooden door. She knocked quietly.

"Come in," a caring voice answered, sounding soft and gentle even through the wood. She opened the door and was almost knocked over for a second time by the executive, who had to lean forward so as not to hit his head on the rounded header to the door. The room was the simple monk's living quarters, a single room on the ground floor with only one window overlooking a lively, colorful flower garden. With the three of them in it, there was little room to move. The executive looked around the room, aware that the lobby of his office was twenty-five times larger than this man's dwelling.

The monk looked up from his desk and smiled warmly. "May I help you?"

"I'm here to talk to you about my soul. It's empty and dry," said the executive, getting right to the point. He assumed that both men were too busy for small talk.

"Thank you, Alice," said the monk, as the woman left.

"Oh...yes, thank you," The executive's voice caught in his throat for a moment as Alice smiled at the two of them and shut the door, leaving them alone.

"Sit down, please," said the monk with a calmness in his voice that the executive had never heard from anyone in his business office.

The busy man sat down on a simple chair, glancing quickly at his watch.

"Tell me your story," said the monk in a kind voice. "And please don't worry about the time; take as much as you need."

The busy executive started by telling him about yesterday's canceled appointment and his hour alone with only his thoughts. He told of what he had discovered about the inside of him and the relationships outside of him. The monk looked at the executive as if he had all the time in the world.

The executive talked until he felt the other man understood where he was coming from, and the monk listened quietly, nodding his head with compassion and understanding.

When the man was done talking about the condition of his soul, the monk excused himself and left the small room for a few moments before returning with a small pouch.

"I think your soul is dry simply because you haven't given it anything to drink. I think you are now finding yourself with no spring to draw from, no rich soil to grow in, no sunlight to warm your heart, and no quietness for your mind to find its way."

Those simple words felt too light, in his world full of meetings and deadlines, cut-and-dry conversations, and no time to waste, the monks' words were full of gentle truth. The executive knew the other man was right.

"I think you may find that after years of neglecting your soul, it is even emptier than you think, but you will find that out for yourself soon enough. I am glad you are here."

The monk held the pouch in his palm and shook it a little, the smooth stones inside clacking together softly.

"Inside the pouch are seven stones. Each stone has something written on it that I would like you to do," said the monk as he set the pouch down.

"Once you've experienced the assignment on a stone, you can then draw out another stone. All I ask is that you don't move on to the next stone until you have fed your soul from each new experience; you can wait as long as you need between each stone until you're ready for the next one. I would like for you to replace each stone with a symbol, an icon to remind you of what you have learned. When you're done, there will be no stones in the bag and only seven memories of your journey to feed your soul."

The executive looked at the brown leather bag, and when he looked back at the monk, he was gone.

The First Smooth Stone

The man reached his hand slowly into the pouch and pulled out an ordinary stone the size of a golf ball. He realized quickly that by putting the assignments on stones and not on a list, this experience would be random. Even the monk had no idea what order the man would be doing things.

He had a lot of urgent things to do back at the office before this day was over, so he wanted to get the task the monk had given him, complete it, and be on his way.

He looked down at the stone and read, "BE STILL."

"That's it," he sighed, "Two words with no instructions." He sat there, still for a moment, looking around the room. The room was bare, no magazines to read, and no television to watch while he was "being still."

*What do people do when they are still? H*e thought. He had no idea what to do with the stillness or how long to be still. He sat back in the chair that was almost too small for him and studied the bare walls, bouncing his leg as he looked around. He wondered if his soul was as barren as this room. He'd spent his life filling his office, house, and career with things, now it seemed it was time to fill his soul. *But how and with what...* he thought, his leg still bouncing.

Even though the room was bare, it seemed noisy. He soon realized the noise was actually in his head. He couldn't believe it, how real and urgent they all sounded. All he could hear were voices reminding him of urgent deadlines, unfinished projects, upcoming appointments, and impossible problems. Every voice was clamoring for his attention, loud and unwavering.

"Maybe this is the lesson I am to learn." He stated, feeling a little foolish as he spoke aloud to an empty room. Was that his voice? It sounded so small despite the close quarters. He wanted to pull out another stone and be on with the project, but he remembered the monk told him to stay with each stone until he had experienced it. He could feel he wasn't done and stayed in the chair.

He sat still; it seemed to drag for a long while, so he glanced at his watch and realized he had been there only eighteen minutes.

He tapped his fingers and continued to sit, glancing at his watch now and again. At first, it took all the self-discipline he had to stay put, but over time it became the right thing to do. The executive exhaled softly through his nose and noticed the sunlight filtering in through the wooden blinds, feeling slightly more comfortable in the silence.

In the stillness, he began to hear over the nagging voices of his business world and heard another, deeper voice revealing to him his fears, needs, and dreams. He was surprised at the softness in the voice and how it made his heart quicken for a beat.

Suddenly his phone buzzed in his pocket, and the moment was ripped away. He realized the chair he was on was getting too hard for him. He stood, brushed himself off, and went over to sit on the edge monk's bed. He discovered quickly that the bed wasn't much softer than the chair. However, he stayed on the bed thinking and feeling in the 'here and now' of this moment. That was unusual for him because he always prided himself on living his life a few steps ahead of everyone else. "That's how you win," he had always thought.

As he began to settle back into the silence, his eyes wandered again, and he noticed a little plaque on the wall. How had he missed it? It simply read, "Be still and know that I am God." He knew that he lived his life as if *he* was god, that he was in control, that it was all up to him, and no one else.

But in that stillness, he began to think about God. The man in the sky, a character in the Bible stories he used to read to his children. The longer he was there in the stillness, the more he sensed he was not alone in the room. He had never sensed God in any room with him before, not in his office, not in his home, and sadly not even in the church. But today, he believed God was with him, and that thought brought up feelings both forgotten and genuine. He discovered that those forgotten feelings had always been with him, buried by the constant hustle of his life. There was a God, and it certainly wasn't him. Today was proof of that. He'd come here to fill his soul because he realized he couldn't do it by himself.

"When a man quits believing in God, he becomes God, and he doesn't make a very good one."

The brief, quiet time allowed him to find the space he needed to listen to not only what was going on in his life, but if he was quiet enough, maybe hear from God himself.

The days following his visit started more difficult than he imagined. Every time he stopped to take a moment to be still. Another phone would ring, or his assistant would buzz in another appointment. At home, responsibilities stopped him from being still. It wasn't long before he was running again, still only when he slept his few meager hours.

But after a few days, the executive learned to silence his cell phone and let emails sit in his inbox for a while before replying. He even told his assistant to leave ten minutes between each appointment so he could sit in stillness and remember who God was.

Over the coming weeks, he discovered that even when he found quiet moments, the mental stillness was harder to achieve. He struggled with boredom in the stillness. He found himself facing his own emptiness, asking questions he had no answers to, and discovering the ghosts that drove his story. He would have quite the journey had he not felt a weight in his chest when he thought about abandoning his project.

The next month he went to see the monk, not for another stone, but to dive deeper into the truth of the one he carried. When he sought the monk, he always had time to listen to him, but rather than counsel him, the monk would ask him a question to reflect on while he was there.

The man discovered over time, that stillness was a discipline, not easily lived in a noisy, hurried world. When lost, humans seemed to run faster rather than slow down and ask for directions. Over time, the man not only found the monastery a quiet place to reflect, but he found other places in his world: a living room without his television on, his library at home during the weekends, the long walk to his office with a cup of coffee.

One day he discovered that being 'still' wasn't so much his body as his soul. When he focused on his soul, he found he was more worried and agitated than he had been aware. He slowly learned to hand that worry and agitation over to a God who was willing to accept it from him.

One day in the middle of a meeting that wasn't going in the right direction, he reached into his briefcase and felt the round, smooth stone. The man leaned back in his chair and, while listening to the chaos, found himself smiling on the inside. The problem they were dealing with was one that God would solve in His time. After the meeting, one of his assistants grabbed the executive on his way out and said, "I have never seen you at so much peace, is everything okay?"

"All is well," responded the man with a smile on his face.

He now sensed it was the right time to discover the secret of nurturing his soul in a new way, and the next week the man drove back to the monastery. The monk wasn't in his room, but the small satchel of stones was lying on the bed, waiting for him to return in time.

He put the stone on the monk's bed and replaced it with an old phone charger, reminding him that being still was something he still had to actively focus on, but he has found comfort in the quiet times. He reached into the bag and wondered where the journey would lead him next.

The Second Smooth Stone

Standing in the monks' simple room, he pulled the second stone out of the leather pouch and looked down on it, laying in the palm of his hand. The words "MEDITATE ON SCRIPTURE" were written on it. He rolled the stone around between his fingers, trying to understand what this would mean to him.

The executive hadn't read the Bible since he was a child, he didn't even know if he *had* a Bible anymore. He knew his wife had one, but that didn't help him here. Looking around the room, he noticed an old worn leather Bible falling apart from heavy use on the bedside table. The man picked it up and studied the worn cover, noting that the monk had to use it every day for it to be so beaten up. "I have no idea where to start reading." He leafed through the book several times, careful with the frail pages. Still, several fell out, and he reached down, picked them up and slid them back into where he thought they belonged.

He sat down on the bed, confused about what to do next. A thought from his former exercise popped into his head, "Be Still and know that I am God". He once again sat in the quiet room, and his trail of thought led him toward a recent funeral for a dear friend, and the pastor read from Psalm 23. The passage had something to do with comfort. It was his only lead, so he took it and began to look for the passage. He was surprised that he found it rather quickly, right in the middle of the book. Smiling softly to himself, he scanned the passage, "*Nice themes to live by,*" he thought.

He laid down the Bible back down on the lampstand and stood, beginning to make his way to the door when he stopped. Something tugged at the back of his mind, and he turned back, picked up the Bible, and this time read the passage very slowly.

He looked at it differently this time, and so he read it a third time, this time reading it out loud, reflecting on every word. The man went over to the desk where the monk had been sitting when they first met each other and sat, his mind focused on the shepherd in this passage.

Who is the shepherd? He thought, glancing at the other Psalms on the page.

"The Lord...The Lord is the shepherd. *My* shepherd."

The truth of the first line made the man realize that he didn't have a shepherd looking over him—he was alone in his world. With that realization in mind, he read the passage again and began to understand the wonderful things the Shepherd did for his sheep: He made them rest, restored their soul, led them to water, and the list went on. The man wondered how different his life would be if he had the Shepherd do that for him.

He had been walking in a slow path from the door to the desk. Even though it was early in the morning, he sighed and sat on the end of the monk's bed, realizing how tired he was. He scanned the verses over and over, reflecting on each one. What surprised him was no matter how many times he read a verse, there was something more to be discovered; a different question, a different word to focus on, and a new truth to be found. Having read that psalm so many times, he began to experience a deep assurance. For the first time, he felt as if he wasn't alone, that there was someone looking after him, taking care of him, who had his best interest in mind.

In his life, he operated under the presupposition that the only person looking after him was himself. He pushed, shoved, manipulated, oversold, over-promised, and overworked because he *had* to. He thought if he didn't, no one else would look after his interest.

In that little room, he learned something new; he learned someone else was looking out for him.

He stood to leave the monk's room when he remembered he didn't own a Bible. The man pressed a hand to the cover of the Bible on the monk's desk and gave it a pat, slipped his coat on, and headed toward the monastery's exit. There, on a small stand beside the door, was a shelf full of Bibles, and in neat handwriting, he read "Take One." He chose one from the end of the shelf, newer and slimmer than the monk's book.

That week, the busy man took ten minutes in the morning while waiting for his coffee to brew, and read the Bible from the monastery. He began at the beginning of the Psalms and discovered how dynamically it was written: with chapters about being comforted, being afraid, being in awe, and just being thankful for everything in life.

By the end of the week, the man was almost sad to return and give back the Bible. He had found peace while reading those passages, something which he had never felt reading business reports or the *New York Times*.

When he arrived, he found the monk's room the same as the week before, empty, except for the small bag of stones on the bed. But this time, there was a note there too, "Consider the Bible a gift."

This week, he discovered something that he didn't think existed; a caring God, a shepherd, and he smiled. The man placed the band of an old watch into the bag with his phone charger, reminding him that his time with God was becoming more precious to him than time spent in his office.

The Third Smooth Stone

The man reached in for the third stone, which read "EXPERIENCE NATURE." He nodded down at the stone and looked out the window, noticed beyond the flower garden a gated archway. On the other side of the archway set in the stone wall was a pathway that went into the forest behind the monastery.

He left the monks' room and walked through the courtyard to the gate, glancing around to see if anyone was out here already. No one was, and he tentatively opened the gate, not wanting to somehow ruin the quiet moment.

He passed the threshold slowly at first, noticing his instinct was to get somewhere fast. But, he remembered that the assignment was not about going, it was about the experience.

When was the last time I have walked anywhere without a destination in mind? He thought, shielding his eyes with a hand to scan the treeline. Life to him was about arriving, not enjoying. He was the kind of man his family hated to go on vacations with because he was always in a hurry; to him, there was never time to stop and look at the ocean with his sons, never time to stop at a roadside diner and have coffee and pie with his wife, never time to take the scenic route and discover something new along the way.

It had been years since he had walked on anything but concrete, his landscape team took care of his lawn at home.

"For that matter," he spoke softly as he watched his expensive leather shoes hit the edge of the grass, "it feels like it's been years since I've walked on anything but my stair stepper in the gym."

There was no time in life for a walk that would take him somewhere without business involved. This man's whole life was about getting everything he could out of time. People paid him a lot for his time, and he wasn't going to waste it.

However, as he walked, he was caught off guard by the beauty of the flowers along the path. They seem to come up out of the ground so naturally and, while his office had flowers, all he noticed were their expensive containers, not what was in them. He glanced around once and made himself stop and take a long inhale of the floral air around him. Such a simple act that he thought he had no time for. He smelled one flower after another, each breath bringing him pleasure.

Once he opened his eyes, his breath was taken by the pine trees as they reached to the sky and beyond. They were massive, calling his gaze even farther upward into the clear blue of the afternoon. At that moment, a breeze came through the trees and filled his lungs with fresh air, his mind clear, and in the moment for the first time in forever.

The path he took turned and ushered him to a meadow clearing that was circled by snow–capped mountains. He was caught off guard by how grand the mountains were, silent and powerful giants. Without regard for his suit, he pulled his slacks up and sat cross-legged in the tall grass by the creek that ran through the green meadow. He had an expensive carpet in his family room, but it felt nothing like this. He heard birds singing, they must have been singing all along, but this was the first time he had heard them.

On the other side of the creek was a family of geese. The two parents herding their six goslings around, making sure they were safe and well cared for. One parent led them into the water, and the other one followed them in, honking as they swam in a line. He couldn't help but wonder when the last time his whole family was together like that.

He wondered how many meals his kids had with only one parent home, how many took place in front of their television set. His kids were growing, and he wasn't a part of their story...Too many late-night dinners, too many plane trips, and his family had decided that there were only three of them, not four.

He continued to sit by the creek in the meadow, finding his throat tight from the sight before him and the feelings he was slowly unraveling. He enjoyed the sounds of the water, the feel of the grass, and the smell of the flowers. They fed his soul, and he felt more alive than ever, even well-rested.

There was a creator, he thought as he took in the scene. *A creator who had created all this.* Buildings had led him to believe in man; mountains led him to believe in God.

A sudden thought passed his mind as he watched the creek flow, had the shepherd led him here? He remembered the psalm he read earlier, *He makes me lie down in green pastures, He restores my soul.*

Walking back to the monastery, he enjoyed the greens, reds, blues, and yellows of nature. The city was filled with shades of gray, but nature had revealed a pallet of colors that was the envy of any artist. He realized he was spending too much time reading black type on white legal paper, he needed color in his soul. And so, before he pulled the next stone from the pouch, he removed his silk pocket square and walked back outside, the sun hitting him warmly on the back. He gathered a handful of rich soil and dropped it into the center of the fabric, setting a fallen leaf on top. The man tied it tight and returned to the monks' room, where he swapped the bundle of earth for the next stone. It was one of the best trades of his life.

His drive home was slower, quieter. He rolled down his tinted windows and let the sunset paint the interior of his car. His shoes had dirt on them, he was down a pocket square, but he felt as light as the clouds that followed him home. Every day that week, he no longer ordered his lunch to be delivered to his office or drove his clients to expensive restaurants in dark cars. Instead, he left his office at noon and walked down to where he would eat. If he had clients, he brought them along for the walk. And every day, the man was sure to walk through the nearest park where, for a few minutes, he felt like he was back in the meadow of the monastery.

The Fourth Smooth Stone

When he arrived back at the courtyard of the monastery the next week, he knew what he would find in the room. He immediately reached for the bag to get the fourth stone, which read "LISTEN TO MUSIC." He walked back into the monastery, not knowing how that was going to be done here. He doubted they had any kind of music besides their hymnal books, but who knew. This stone went hand in hand with the last one, but music was well, just music. Nature was always in motion, and since he had stopped to notice, always astonishing.

As he approached a small sanctuary at the back of the monastery, he heard what sounded like a choir singing beautiful, simple chants. If he remembered anything from school, it sounded like they were singing in Latin. It was fresh and new to him, and it made him want to sit and listen, nothing like the bass-heavy music at parties he often heard.

All the music in his life was noisy, wordy, and loud. These soft sounds soothed his soul and blanketed his heart with peace. He entered the small sanctuary and looked around, seeing a choir of six monks on a simple stage. The man watched the conductor, his hands waving in seamless time with the chants. As the hymn ended softly, the conductor turned to the back of the room. "You are welcome to stay if you wish to, my friend."

"Thank you very much," the executive said as he slid into one of the wooden pews and listened to the choir start again. Over time he looked up at the tall ceiling that gave him the opportunity to be fully encased in the music, peace settling in his soul. He closed his eyes, and the music took him to places he had never been, places of peace within himself, places he didn't even know existed.

The music cascaded down his soul as if it was a waterfall. His life was nothing like this music; it was, in fact, the opposite. This music invited him to think thoughts he hadn't thought before. It reminded him about the good in his life rather than the bad, about hope more than problems, and about love more than anger. The song currently reminded the man of a Christmas song, which lightened his heart for a moment. He thought this music sounded special and holy, a kind of music that he soon believed more people should enjoy.

He was surprised at what the music did for his soul. He had always enjoyed his radio on the way to work, the music, news, and talk shows. However, the noise always seemed to leave him more frustrated and angry. His old music helped him find an escape, and he still enjoyed what was played on the radio or various genres that were popular.

This music, though, this music was different. It was leading him into a deeper life, and it began to bring a different layer of peace, one not brought by anything before. The music was, in fact, another avenue, another spring from which his soul could drink.

The afternoon went by quickly as he sat and listened to the singers' practice, a moment the man had never experienced before. When the music stopped, he stood up and clapped, the choir blinking at him as the director smiled. The man thanked the group for their lovely performance and strolled out of the sanctuary.

He knew this week was going to be an easy task, but it would take time. When he returned home, he began researching various kinds of chants and what they usually sang about. He would make it a point during his nature walks to add a few chants and some more classical pieces into his queue, adding a layer of appreciation for the day. A lot of the pop playlists he threw on were filled with empty lyrics with an excellent beat. There would always be a time and place for fun music like that, but every time a chant or classical piece came on, his soul would find a few more minutes of peace.

He had his new music with him wherever he went, in his office, at home, in his car. When he returned to the monastery at the end of the week, he brought with him his favorite pair of headphones. Whenever he had to travel for work, his headphones would never leave his ears. They kept him in a bubble, but he felt lighter as he placed them into the pouch. Music was good, but conversations and connections were good too.

The Fifth Smooth Stone

He reached into the pouch and pulled out the fifth stone, with "SERVE OTHERS" written on it. He looked around for someone he could possibly serve, but he neither could see nor hear anyone.

He started walking down the hallway, not as familiar with the inside of the monastery as the outside. There was a slight bounce to his step as he walked about, more excited than nervous. Given what he had experienced so far, he wasn't afraid but energized. In these months, he had learned more than he had in his whole life. It had become an adventure to live fully, not to be in the fast lane but to take time to focus on new things, to live in new ways.

As he walked down the hallway, he noticed a kitchen, and in it was an elderly woman washing a mountain of dishes. She was the same one he met when he first came into the monastery, the woman with the beautiful smile...*Alice!*

He smiled and knocked on the open door, "Excuse me, may I help you with those?"

The woman smiled at him, her eyes tired. "Oh, no thank you, I'm fine."

"It's no trouble, that's far too big of a job for just one person."

"If you insist, thank you very much."

He couldn't remember the last time he had washed dishes, or for that matter, helping someone without expecting something in return.

Neither of them said anything for a while until she spoke, "Have you enjoyed your stay here?"

The man thought for a moment as he dried a plate and placed it on a nearby shelf, "Yes, I really have."

They continued washing and drying the dishes in silence, each reflecting on themselves in a quiet moment.

He soon looked at her and asked, "Would you mind telling me your story? I mean, what brought you to this quiet place?"

The elderly lady smiled, nodded softly, and told him a story he would never forget.

She told of being born in an orphanage in Romania and how she didn't know her parents or what had ever become of them. When she was there, the orphanage was bombed during the Second World War, killing all of the adults that had helped them. She remembered how several older children tried to care for the younger ones, all living a year off of roots and scraps that were found around the orphanage.

"Half of the children in the orphanage died that year." She wiped at her eyes with the corner of her apron, and the man found himself getting misty-eyed.

When she was sixteen years old, she left the orphanage and moved into a small one-bedroom apartment in Budapest with six other girls. They all worked as maids in the big city. Life was hard, her first job lasted several months, but she was never paid for her work. When she complained, they kicked her out.

He stood there, washing the larger pans, and realized his story was not nearly as painful as hers. She seemed to have risen above, and her experiences had led her to such a rich soul. His wealth had somehow taken him down a different path to a poor soul.

She went on to tell him how she had married an American soldier who brought her back to the United States. They were happy until he died in an automobile accident soon after she had given birth to their first child, a boy.

She never remarried, and their young son soon lost his fight with a rare sickness. She decided to move to this monastery soon after, wanting to feel at peace once again.

Her story was bleak, but she told it with such joy. He couldn't believe what had happened to her and he couldn't believe the peaceful, grateful spirit she had. In helping her, he had been helped. She thanked him for helping, smiled, and made her way out of the kitchen and down the hallway to make beds.

He reached down and grabbed the gold pin on his tie, one he received in some corporate meeting long ago. He recalled how his boss told him how much his story touched him, how genuine and powerful it was. The man believed him then, but now? Alice's story will stay with him forever. He returned to the monks' room and placed his tie pin in the leather pouch. He kept the stone in his palm, and before leaving, he placed the stone in the windowsill over the large empty sink.

That day, he walked back to his car, humbled. How could he have been so selfish in his life to never serve someone or listen to their own story? As he neared the busy city, he thought of ways to continue to serve others.

That week, he learned there were many different ways to serve other people in his daily life. Serving someone didn't always mean doing hard work for someone, but it was doing little acts of kindness for no other reason than to see a person smile. He surprised his secretaries with their morning coffees, held doors for everyone in his office, and initiated conversations at his dinner table.

Things are definitely healing.

The Sixth Smooth Stone

When the man pulled into the small monastery lot, he wanted to find Alice and thank her for all she had taught him about service; he looked for her in the kitchen and the main room but couldn't find her, so he went down the hall and knocked before entering the monks' room. The pouch was at the foot of the bed today, and he felt around for his sixth stone. Pulling the second to last stone from the pouch, it read, "ENJOY ART."

Nature, music, and now art… The man tossed the stone in the air and caught it swiftly, walking back to the main room of the monastery. He made a left instead of a right and found a room with an open door. Inside the room, there was a chair, a few candles glowing softly, and a painting on the wall. He looked about before walking inside, the small room quiet and cool.

The man had never seen a painting like this before, but it was a lovely, peaceful scene. He relaxed into the chair as he studied the two figures. The soft oils and rich details made it look like a window to another world. He soon stood and rolled his shoulders, stiff from sitting so long. He did not know that time it was, but he could see from the small window on the opposite wall that it was starting to get dark outside. But, something drew him back to the painting. *Enjoy art…*

He took a step back and noticed how large the frame was, three feet wide by four feet high. He sighed through his nose and studied a little harder, feeling as if he was soon standing by the people in the picture.

The main figure was a woman standing by a well and the other, a man, sat on the opposite side. The painting was mostly in shades of browns, greens, and yellows reflecting the edge of a desert the two people were in. The sitting man was in a red robe with a blue sash, rather striking despite being in the shade.

The two figures were alone by the well, and the woman looked tired, like someone who had lived a difficult life. She looked on the younger scale, but her posture and clothes reflected her working-class lifestyle.

Life had not been easy to this woman, the executive thought.

The shadows on the ground indicated it was noon, and the executive could see a city in the background of the picture, was it hers or his? He thought it was odd it was just the two of them, they didn't seem to be a couple. The man looked closer at the bucket in the woman's right hand, noticing the man had nothing in his hands, but they were raised as if he were speaking. *What were they talking about? The temperature? The long walk from the city?* The executive continued to look, soon noticing that her body was turned back to the city as if she was turning to leave. Her bucket was still empty, so why would she leave?

The sound of shuffling brought the man to reality, a younger monk entering the room with his eyes on a book. He glanced up and smiled, the book closing silently. "I'm sorry, I didn't know anyone was here."

"That's okay," answered the man, running a hand through his hair.

The monk turned to leave, but before he was out of the room, the executive stopped him, "Excuse me, could you tell me who the man is in this painting?"

"That's Jesus with the woman at the well; it's based on the story in the Gospel of John when Jesus met a woman at the well in Jericho."

The monk bid the man goodnight, the busy man barely hearing it as he looked back at the picture.

"Jesus." He said simply, his throat tightening at the name.

He swallowed and stepped up to the picture, feeling a little weak. Jesus was pointing to himself, the woman gazing at him. The man tapped at his coat and took his Bible from an outside pocket, looking happily worn. He flipped through the pages and found the book of John, chapter four: "Jesus Talks With the Samaritan Woman."

He read the passage quietly, his eyes moving from the pages to the painting. "Living water…" The executive breathed, his grip on his Bible tight. Jesus was explaining how He could provide, be the source of water for her soul. For his soul? He was thirsty, his soul yearning to be entirely full. The man could relate to the woman, realizing he too had come to this retreat to hide from others, to find the source, the well.

Warm tears rolled down the executive's face as he closed his Bible, giving a silent prayer for this moment and this painting. The tears touched his dry, barren soul and a weight lifted from his shoulders as he exited the room. He made his way to the monks' room, and without a second thought, he retrieved his first business card, something he had carried with him for years and placed it into his pouch.

The Seventh Smooth Stone

He could have left now his life would be forever changed, but there was one more stone. He reached his hand in and pulled out the seventh stone that read, "KEEP LIFE SIMPLE."

He looked at the monk's quarters he had stood in, month after month, and cracked a smile. Through all of the stones and their lessons, above all else, this was still a simple room. The man sat down on the only chair in the room, hard as the day he first sat on it. He recalled a meeting in his office last week, how twenty representatives easily fit at his table, laughing during the mandated post-meeting break time the executive had put in place.

How could he make his life as simple as this man's room? He knew he had to simplify his life, but there were so many directions he could go. What things was he going to leave behind, and what was he going to keep? Everything in his life seemed to bring more frustration than happiness, but he also remembered the pouch that held a reminder of all his lessons. Everything that he thought would make his life easier made it more crowded, more complex and everything he bought eventually broke. The bag now held his old life, and he was determined to let the past go.

He took out his wallet and began to clean it out. It was far too thick to be in a back pocket: He would give a donation for the monk and his books, for the Bibles, for the flower garden, for the choir, for Alice's kitchen, and for the art. The man began to take everything out and make piles on the bed.

"Too many credit cards and too few pictures of my family." He only put back what he now knew he needed, not what he wanted.

The man then felt his keys in his pocket, weighing much more than he thought. He counted twelve, shaking his head down at the bundle. Too many to have, too many things to own, too many things to worry about. What did he really need? A door key, an office key, and a car key. He took all the clutter from his key ring, leaving only the three keys and his favorite keychain, a simple metal bar that had his wedding date stamped onto it.

He began to think of the other areas in his life that needed simplifying as he drove home: possessions scattered around his house and his office. He mentally made a list in his mind about the clutter in his life, and how he could use what he didn't need to bless others. Upon arriving home, he saw books and movies, furniture and clothes, all material goods he believed would give him joy.

The week started at home as he removed items that he never used or no longer needed, donating them to various charities and thrift stores in the area. Instead of three sets of fine china, he kept his wife's favorite set of everyday dishware and even found his old favorite coffee mug.

This same method of simplifying was also used in his office. He rearranged the art on his walls, kept his windows open, and even added a few potted plants around the room. While it looked less modern, the additions made him smile and would remind him of the stones. By the end of the week, he felt less cluttered and noticed new freedom settle over his life. When he arrived at the monastery the following week, he wondered if he would find the monk in his room this time. As he stuck his head into different rooms and waved at the now familiar faces, he prayed for each of them in turn, feeling comfortable in his daily talk with God.

Once he greeted everyone and made his way outside, he finally found the monk watering a small bed of roses under his window. The leather pouch that once held the stones now rested against the monk's hip, the last stone in the hand of the executive. The man had found an old schedule of his, a mere few weeks before he met the monk, and had folded it as small as it could get.

The calendar days of his old life were always full of unnecessary, and as he gave the stone and the folded paper to the monk, he let out a final sigh. The monk smiled at the man, put the paper into the pouch, and the stone in his pocket. He continued watering, moving to the flowers that surrounded the roses. Both men enjoyed the quiet moment, birdsong echoing through the garden. After a beat, the monk wiped his hands on his robe and turned to the man with the pouch in hand.

"What is in your pouch?" asked the monk. The man took the pouch and opened it, explaining each item and how his life had changed for the better.

"Very good," said the monk, smiling widely at the man. "Please don't forget what you learned, my friend. Reflect on that bag, apply what you have learned, and praise the Lord. Do these things, and your soul will be full."

The man took a long way home, the leather pouch sitting in the passenger seat. He knew the secret to a full soul wasn't in the bag, but the lessons he had learned from within.

As he drove, he smiled.

The End

www.ingramcontent.com/pod-product-compliance
Lightning Source LLC
Chambersburg PA
CBHW022055170626
46808CB00003B/1477